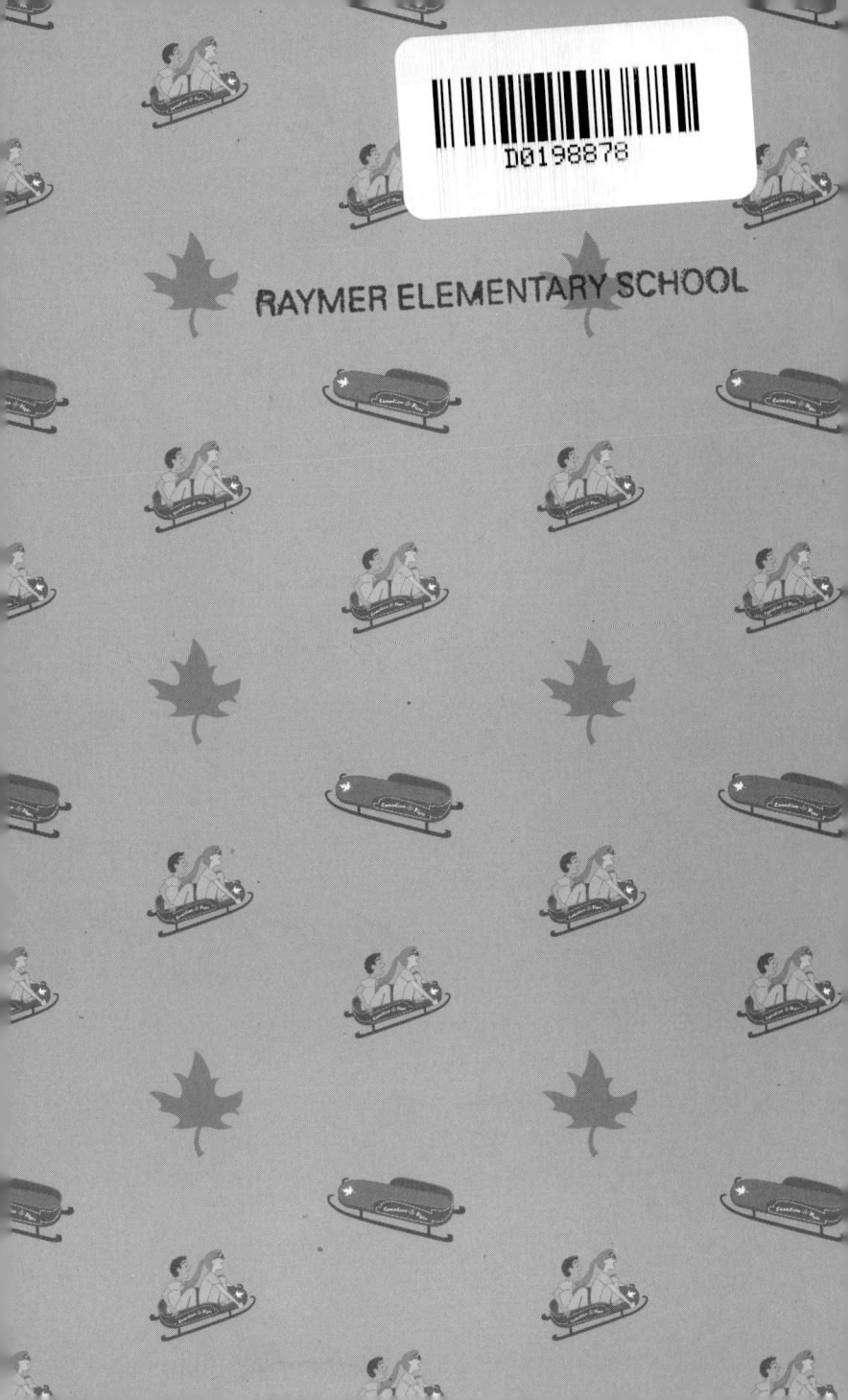

RAYMER ELEMENTARY SCHOOL

Teachers, librarians, and kids
from across Canada are talking about
Canadian Flyer Adventures.
Here's what some of them had to say:

Great Canadian historical content, excellent illustrations,
and superb closing historical facts (I love the kids'
commentary!). ~ *SARA S., TEACHER, ONTARIO*

As a teacher–librarian I welcome this series with open
arms. It fills the gap for Canadian historical adventures
at an early reading level! There's fast action, interesting,
believable characters, and great historical information.
~ *MARGARET L., TEACHER–LIBRARIAN, BRITISH COLUMBIA*

The *Canadian Flyer Adventures* will transport young
readers to different eras of our past with their appealing
topics. Thank goodness there are more artifacts in that old
dresser ... they are sure to lead to even more escapades.
~ *SALLY B., TEACHER–LIBRARIAN, MANITOBA*

When I shared the book with a grade 1–2 teacher at
my school, she enjoyed the book, noting that her students
would find it appealing because of the action-adventure
and short chapters. ~ *HEATHER J., TEACHER AND
LIBRARIAN, NOVA SCOTIA*

Newly independent readers will fly through
each *Canadian Flyer Adventure*, and be asking for
the next installment! Children will enjoy the fast-paced
narrative, the personalities of the main characters, and
the drama of the dangerous situations the children
find themselves in. ~ *PAM L., LIBRARIAN, ONTARIO*

I love the fact that these are Canadian adventures—kids should know how exciting Canadian history is. Emily and Matt are regular kids, full of curiosity, and I can see readers relating to them. ~ *JEAN K., TEACHER, ONTARIO*

What kids told us:

I would like to have the chance to ride on a magical sled and have adventures. ~ *EMMANUEL*

I would like to tell the author that her book is amazing, incredible, awesome, and a million times better than any book I've read. ~ *MARIA*

I would recommend the *Canadian Flyer Adventures* series to other kids so they could learn about Canada too. The book is just the right length and hard to put down. ~ *PAUL*

The books I usually read are the full-of-fact encyclopedias. This book is full of interesting ideas that simply grab me. ~ *ELEANOR*

At the end of the book Matt and Emily say they are going on another adventure. I'm very interested in where they are going next! ~ *ALEX*

I like when Emily and Matt fly into the sky on a sled towards a new adventure. I can't wait for the next book! ~ *JI SANG*

Pioneer Kids

Frieda Wishinsky

Illustrated by Dean Griffiths

Maple Tree is an imprint of Owlkids Books Inc.
10 Lower Spadina Avenue, Suite 400, Toronto, Ontario M5V 2Z2
www.owlkidsbooks.com

Text © 2007 Frieda Wishinsky   Illustrations © 2007 Dean Griffiths

Distributed in Canada by University of Toronto Press
5201 Dufferin Street, Toronto, Ontario M3H 5T8

Distributed in the United States by Publishers Group West
1700 Fourth Street, Berkeley, California 94710

Dedication
With thanks to Georgette and Eric Levine

Acknowledgements
Many thanks to the hard-working Maple Tree team—Sheba Meland, Anne Shone, Grenfell
Featherstone, Deborah Bjorgan, Cali Hoffman, Dawn Todd, and Erin Walker—for their insightful
comments and steadfast support. Special thanks to Dean Griffiths and Claudia Dávila for their
engaging and energetic illustrations and design.

Cataloguing in Publication Data
Wishinsky, Frieda
Pioneer kids / Frieda Wishinsky ; illustrated by Dean Griffiths.

(Canadian flyer adventures ; 6)
ISBN 978-1-897349-04-5 (bound)
ISBN 978-1-897349-05-2 (pbk.)

1. Frontier and pioneer life—Saskatchewan—Juvenile fiction.
I. Griffiths, Dean, 1967– II. Title. III. Series: Wishinsky, Frieda. Canadian flyer adventures ; 6.

PS8595.I834P46 2007   jC813'.54   C2007-901863-7

Library of Congress Control Number: 2007939911

Design & art direction: Claudia Dávila

 Canadian Heritage / Patrimoine canadien   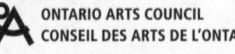 Canada   Ontario — Ontario Media Development Corporation

 Canada Council for the Arts / Conseil des Arts du Canada   ONTARIO ARTS COUNCIL / CONSEIL DES ARTS DE L'ONTARIO   Société de développement de l'industrie des médias de l'Ontario

We acknowledge the financial support of the Canada Council for the Arts, the Ontario Arts Council,
the Government of Canada through the Canada Book Fund (CBF) and the Government of Ontario
through the Ontario Media Development Corporation's Book Initiative for our publishing activities.

Printed in Canada

B   C   D   E   F

CONTENTS

HOW IT ALL BEGAN

Emily and Matt couldn't believe their luck. They discovered an old dresser full of strange objects in the tower of Emily's house. They also found a note from Emily's Great-Aunt Miranda: "The sled is yours. Fly it to wonderful adventures."

They found a sled right behind the dresser! When they sat on it, shimmery gold words appeared:

> *Rub the leaf*
> *Three times fast.*
> *Soon you'll fly*
> *To the past.*

The sled rose over Emily's house. It flew over their town of Glenwood. It sailed out of a cloud and into the past. Their adventures on the flying sled had begun! Where will the sled take them next? Turn the page to find out.

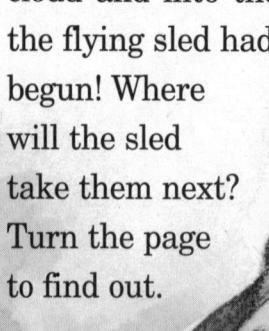

1

Surprise! Surprise!

"Come on, Matt! Let's fly high!" shouted Emily, pumping hard on her swing.

Emily and Matt soared above the bushes in Emily's yard.

"I can see a bird building a nest in our maple tree!" she called.

"I can see a cat with a dead mouse in its mouth in my yard," said Matt.

"That's gross!"

"It's not as gross as T-rex eating a dead Lambeosaurus in dinosaur times. Remember?"

Emily shuddered. How could she forget? Matt loved dinosaurs. He'd chosen their second adventure on the magic sled, and they'd flown to dinosaur times. Now it was Matt's turn to choose again.

"Where do you want to go this time?" Emily asked.

"Follow me," said Matt, leaping off the swing. "I'll show you."

Emily jumped off, and they hurried inside her house. They raced up the rickety stairs to the tower room.

As soon as they were inside, Matt opened the second drawer of the old dresser. "I'm going to close my eyes and pull something out," he said.

"Wait! You could pull out anything. We could land anywhere...any time. It could be scary."

"We've gone to scary times before, and we

had fun. And we've always come back."

Emily sighed. "I guess you're right! Okay, go ahead. Dig in."

Matt closed his eyes and reached inside the drawer. Emily watched as he touched soft things, sharp things, long, bumpy, and round things.

"I think...I think..."

"Come on, Matt. Choose!"

"Okay. Here goes. One. Two. Three." Matt yanked out a round object.

"It's an egg," said Emily.

Matt frowned. "It's an egg, but..."

Emily laughed. "I bet you thought you were pulling out another dinosaur egg, so we would have to go to dinosaur times again."

"Well...," sputtered Matt.

"Well, it isn't a dinosaur egg. Not unless dinosaurs lay fancy, decorated eggs."

The egg in Matt's hand was red, blue, and black, with a beautiful pattern and flowers.

Matt read the label out loud: "Easter Egg, Prairies, 1910."

"There won't be any dinosaurs there," he said.

"But I bet this egg-celent egg will take us on an egg-citing adventure," said Emily.

Matt smiled. "You know. That's eggs-actly what I was thinking, too. Let's go!"

2

Too Hot for Licks

As soon as Matt and Emily hopped on the sled, the shimmery gold words appeared:

Rub the leaf
Three times fast.
Soon you'll fly
To the past.

Matt rubbed the words. Soon they were flying over Emily's house, over Glenwood, and into a fluffy white cloud.

"Hold on! We're going down!" shouted Matt.

The sled burst out of the cloud. It thumped down on the ground. They were surrounded by tall, wavy grass.

Emily and Matt slid off and peered around.

The sky was a clear blue. They could see far into the distance, but there wasn't much to see except sky, sun, grass, and clumps of trees.

"Where are we?" asked Emily.

"I don't know. But we must be in pioneer times. You look like a pioneer girl."

Emily wore a long purple dress with a pinafore, and short brown boots.

"And you look like a pioneer boy."

Matt was dressed in loose brown pants with brown suspenders, a white shirt, and a big tan hat.

"Phew. There's my sketchbook," said Emily, patting her pocket. "Do you have your recorder?"

Matt checked his pockets. "Right here. So, which way should we walk?"

Emily pointed to the right. "How about thataway?"

The sun beat down on their heads as they dragged the sled through the tall grass.

"I wish I was wearing shorts. It's too hot for a long dress," said Emily, wiping her face with the back of her hand.

"Hey, Em. Listen. I think I hear a horse and a dog behind us."

Matt and Emily whirled around. An old wagon came up a rise behind them. A horse pulled the wagon, and a man and a woman sat in front. A large black and white dog yapped and raced around in the back of the wagon.

"Want a lift to school?" asked the man, who was holding the reins.

"Sure," said Emily.

"Hot day for a sled," said the man.

"I know, but we're...," stammered Matt.

"Going to bring something home from school on it," added Emily.

"I see. Hop in!" said the man. "I'm John Johansson, and this is my wife, Karolina. That's Rusty back there, and he loves company."

Emily and Matt climbed into the back of the wagon. Rusty licked Matt hello with his long tongue.

Emily giggled. "Rusty really likes you."

"Go away, Rusty. It's too hot," muttered Matt. He brushed Rusty's face away from his.

But Rusty kept licking Matt's face, ears, and hair.

"I'm going to draw Rusty," said Emily, pulling out her sketchbook. "He's so cute."

"He's not cute. He's annoying and wet," grumbled Matt.

"Rusty!" called Mr. Johansson from the front. "Leave the poor boy alone."

Rusty hung his head and slunk over to a corner of the wagon.

"He looks so sad," said Emily.

"Do you want him to lick you?" asked Matt. "That might cheer him up."

"But it wouldn't cheer me up," said Emily. "His tongue is as long as a salami!"

"School's coming up!" Mr. Johansson called from the front.

Emily and Matt peered ahead. They saw a log building beside a small shed, a lopsided shack, and a rickety barn.

Matt sighed. "Why did you agree to go to school, Em? What kind of adventure is school?"

"School might be fun," said Emily. "Come on. Let's see what happens."

Matt nodded. "All right. At least we'll be out of the sun."

"Here you are," said Mr. Johansson, pulling on the horse's reins. "Now don't give poor Miss Bridges any trouble. She's only been the teacher for two weeks. It's hard getting good teachers way out here."

With that, Mr. Johansson and his wife waved goodbye. Their wagon clattered and clanged away down the dusty road.

3

Big Foot

"Hey, Big Foot!" shouted a red-headed boy riding a black horse.

"Go back to wherever you came from!" shouted a curly-haired boy walking beside him.

"Who are those boys yelling at?" asked Emily as they neared the school.

"That tall blond boy walking alone," said Matt.

The blond boy's face was beet red. Even his ears were red, but he didn't turn around or say anything. He walked with his head down, staring at the ground.

"Let's hide the sled there," said Matt, pointing to the shed beside the barn. "That way no one will ask any more questions about it."

Emily and Matt ran to the shed. They peeked inside. There wasn't much inside—just old tools and buckets for water. Emily and Matt left the sled and joined the other kids.

Everyone lined up according to size at the front door of the school. Girls lined up on one side, and boys on the other. The tall blond boy, his head still hanging, stood behind a shorter boy.

A young woman hurried out of the school, her long blue skirt swishing as she rang the bell. She wore her brown hair in a tight bun.

"That must be Miss Bridges," whispered Emily.

The children marched into the building. They talked, laughed, and poked each other. Emily and Matt slipped in last and sat across from one another in the back, in the only two seats that were empty.

Matt sat beside the tall blond boy on the boy's side of the room, and Emily sat across the aisle, on the girl's side.

Miss Bridges sat in front at an old wooden desk. On one side of the blackboard, she'd neatly printed the alphabet in large letters.

Miss Bridges folded her hands on the desk. "Please quiet down, children," she said. Her soft words were drowned out by the noise.

She sighed.

Then Miss Bridges stood up and faced the class. "I would like everyone to be quiet," she said more loudly. A few children stopped talking and looked up.

"Did you hear the teacher? Be quiet!" bellowed an older boy in scruffy overalls.

The noise stopped. Miss Bridges cleared her throat.

"Thank you, Isaac. I see we have two new students today." She looked at Matt and Emily.

"I'm Emily Bing."

"I'm Matt Martinez."

"Welcome to our school," said Miss Bridges. "Where do you children live?"

"Far away," said Emily. "We're just visiting for a little while."

"I'm sure you'll become acquainted with all the children in no time."

"Except for the dope beside you," the red-haired boy called out. "He doesn't know how to read and he barely knows how to talk."

He pointed at the blond boy and laughed.

"Yeah. He's dumber than a prairie dog," said his friend.

The blond boy's jaw tightened. He clenched his fists, as if he were about to punch the red-haired boy.

"Luke and Arthur, leave Stefan alone," said Miss Bridges.

"Yes, teacher." Luke spat out the words as if he didn't mean them. Then he poked Arthur and guffawed.

"After we have roll call, I would like you to open your books to page ten. We will recite the poem on the page together," said Miss Bridges. "Emily, I have a book for you. Matt, you will have to share with Stefan. But first I would like you to bow your heads."

The class recited the Lord's Prayer, and then Miss Bridges called attendance.

"Now, let us read the poem," she said.

The children began to recite, but Stefan didn't open his mouth. His face turned red. He stared blankly at the words on the page as if he couldn't read a single one.

4

Squeak, Squeak

After the recitations, Miss Bridges asked the older children to copy the poem onto their slate boards. She asked the younger children to copy alphabet letters that she'd printed on the chalkboard. She gave Emily and Matt slate pencils, which looked like pieces of rock carved long and thin, and a slate board to copy the poem.

Soon the room was filled with the squeaks of the hard pencils against the boards.

"How can they stand all the squeaking?

It gives me a headache," Emily whispered to Matt.

"It's worse than fingernails on a chalk-board," said Matt.

Emily and Matt glanced at Stefan. The squeaks didn't seem to bother him. He copied each letter of the alphabet slowly and carefully.

Miss Bridges walked over to him and put her hand on his shoulder. "How are you doing?" she asked.

Stefan sighed and muttered some words.

"I know you understand almost everything I say, but I wish I could understand what you were saying," said Miss Bridges. "Then I could help you more."

"I understand Stefan," Emily piped up. She didn't know what language he spoke, but she understood it.

"Me too," said Matt.

"You speak Ukrainian?" said Miss Bridges. "That's wonderful."

Emily nodded. So that was the language Stefan spoke. She'd never heard it before, but thanks to the sled's magic, she understood every word!

She turned to Stefan. "Can we help you?" she asked him.

Stefan grinned as if someone had given him a present. "You understand me?" he said to Emily in Ukrainian. "You are Ukrainian, too?"

"No, but we understand you," said Matt. "And we can help you with your printing and reading, if you want."

"Good," said Miss Bridges. "I'll leave you to help Stefan, then." She walked briskly back to her desk, sat down, and busied herself with a pile of paper.

Luke raised his hand. "Teacher, I need to go out," he said.

"Go ahead," said Miss Bridges.

Luke hurried out of the building.

"Where's he going?" Emily whispered to Matt.

Matt pointed out the window to a small lopsided shack. "To the outhouse."

"Outhouse? Oh," said Emily. "They don't have bathrooms, do they?"

"Nope."

"Yuck. That means I have to use the outhouse, too." Emily groaned. She didn't like outhouses. Whenever she went camping, the outhouses were always smelly and full of bugs. She wasn't going to like them any better in pioneer times.

The classroom door opened, and Luke strutted back in.

He passed the back row and jabbed Stefan hard in the ribs.

"Ow!" yelled Stefan.

Luke raised his arm to strike Stefan again. But this time, Stefan grabbed Luke's arm. Luke squirmed and pulled away. As he did, his shirtsleeve ripped.

"Teacher! Teacher!" Luke screamed, pointing to his torn sleeve. "Look what that new boy did. Now he has to pay for my shirt."

5

Say Nothing

"We will discuss this after lunch," said Miss Bridges.

"Miss Bridges," said Emily. "Luke—"

"Not now, Emily. It's time for recess."

Miss Bridges rang the bell. The children trooped outside.

"It's not fair," Emily told Stefan as they headed outside.

Matt nodded. "You only grabbed Luke's arm to stop him from hitting you. You didn't mean to rip his shirt."

"What if they make me pay for the shirt anyway?" said Stefan. "I have no money. My father will be angry. He never wanted me to go to school. He said that I learn enough on the farm."

"Matt and I are going right over to tell Miss Bridges what really happened."

"Please, say nothing. Luke and Arthur will hate me even more if they think I have told on them."

"But you have to stand up to them," said Matt. "We'll help you."

"You don't understand."

"You want to go to school, right?" said Emily.

"Yes. My mother says that learning gives you new chances in life."

"My mom and dad say the same thing," said Matt. "Your mother is right."

"She makes beautiful things, too. Look."

Stefan pulled out a round object covered in a white cotton handkerchief from his knapsack.

"It-it's," stammered Matt.

"It's the egg from the dresser!" said Emily.

"You have seen such an egg before?" asked Stefan.

"We saw one a lot like it," said Matt.

"It's called pysanky. My mother makes it for Easter every year."

"It has so many colours and designs. It's beautiful!" said Emily. "You should show the class."

"What if they laugh? What if they say it's just a stupid egg?"

"Miss Bridges won't laugh, and some of the other kids won't either," said Matt.

Stefan sighed and wrapped his egg again.

"Perhaps, but not now."

Soon Miss Bridges rang the bell to signal the end of recess.

Emily, Matt, and Stefan headed back inside together.

6

The Egg

"Luke and Stefan," said Miss Bridges when they were all seated. "Remember to see me at lunch."

Luke flashed Miss Bridges a sugary smile. "Yes, Miss," he said.

Miss Bridges checked over some papers on her desk. As she did, Luke and Arthur snickered and made faces at Stefan.

Stefan's face turned red but he tried to ignore them.

"We have to do something to help Stefan.

Luke and Arthur won't leave him alone," Matt whispered to Emily.

"I know," said Emily under her breath. "But what?"

"I don't know yet," said Matt as Miss Bridges stood up and faced the class.

"Does anyone have something to show or tell us today?" she asked.

A girl of about six with a blue ribbon in her curly hair raised her hand.

"Come on up, Melanie."

Melanie marched to the front of the class. She showed the class a handkerchief with embroidered flowers. "I made it myself," she said proudly.

"It's lovely," said Miss Bridges.

"Does anyone else have something to show us?"

"Go up," Matt encouraged Stefan.

But Stefan shook his head.

Luke raised his hand. "I have something to show."

"Come on up, Luke."

Luke dug into his beat-up leather pouch and pulled something long and furry out of his bag. He walked to the front.

As he did, Emily pulled out her sketchbook and drew a picture of him clutching the long, furry object in his hand. It was hard to tell what it was.

"I caught a prairie dog eating our carrots," said Luke. "And now I have its tail. Look!"

Luke held up the tail and swung it in the air like a lasso.

Miss Bridges gulped. Then she cleared her throat.

"Thank you. You may sit down, Luke. Anyone else?"

"Come on, Stefan," Emily urged. "We're behind you."

"Okay," said Stefan. "I will show them."

Stefan reached into his knapsack and pulled out the handkerchief-covered egg. Then he raised his hand.

"Stefan! You have something to show us. That's excellent! Please come up," said Miss Bridges smiling.

Stefan walked slowly to the front of the class.

For a minute he looked at all the children. Then he unwrapped the handkerchief and held the egg up.

"My mother made this for Easter," he said in halting English.

"It's beautiful," said Miss Bridges, beaming.

"And I am so delighted you are trying to speak English, Stefan."

"Your mother is talented," said Isaac.

"That egg is pretty," said Melanie. "I wish I could make one."

Stefan's eyes lit up. He carefully rewrapped the egg and began to walk toward his seat. But just before he reached it, Luke stuck his foot straight out into the aisle.

7

Shattered

Emily screamed, "Watch out, Stefan!"

But it was too late. Stefan flew over Luke's foot. He landed face down on the hard dirt floor.

"No! No!" he groaned.

Miss Bridges hurried to his side. "Are you hurt?" she asked as Stefan scrambled to his feet.

"I—I am fine," he muttered in English. "But my—"

He opened his hand.

The beautiful egg was in pieces, shattered like delicate glass.

Stefan swallowed hard. He stared at the eggshells as if he couldn't believe what had happened.

"I'm sorry, Stefan," murmured Miss Bridges. She spun around and glared at Luke. "Why did you deliberately trip Stefan?" Her voice was loud and firm.

"I just stretched my legs, Miss," said Luke. "It was an accident."

"We will speak more about this at lunch," said Miss Bridges sternly. "Class, it is time for arithmetic." Miss Bridges pointed to the blackboard. She had covered it with addition, subtraction, multiplication, and division problems during recess. "Begin."

Then she turned and walked back to her desk.

Stefan wrapped the broken pieces of the egg in the handkerchief. Then he hobbled to his seat.

As he did, Luke snarled, "I'll get you for this."

But Stefan didn't say anything.

It was as if he hadn't heard Luke's words or the threatening tone in his voice. But Emily and Matt heard.

"Did you hear Luke?" whispered Emily.

Matt nodded. "Stefan has to stand up to him, or Luke will never stop bothering him."

Stefan dropped into his seat and slipped the handkerchief into his bag.

Then he picked up his pencil and worked on the math problems.

"Wow! You're fast," whispered Matt as Stefan quickly finished a division problem and zoomed ahead to the next one.

"Numbers are easy for me," Stefan said. "But telling my parents what happened to the egg and Luke's shirt will be hard."

"But it wasn't your fault." said Matt.

"I know, but Mother spent hours decorating the egg with wax and special dyes. I hate Luke and what he has done."

8

Ladies and Gentlemen

"Put away your slate and pencils, class. Line up. It's time for lunch," said Miss Bridges.

The students put down their slates and pulled out their lunch pails. Then they lined up beside the door.

"Luke and Stefan, come to my desk," said Miss Bridges.

Matt patted Stefan on the shoulder. "Good luck," he said.

"Tell Miss Bridges what happened with the shirt. She'll believe you now," said Emily.

"I'll try, but my English is not so good. It will be hard to explain," said Stefan.

"You can call us to come inside and help you," said Matt.

"We'll tell Miss Bridges exactly what happened," said Emily.

"Thank you, but I will try to tell her myself." Stefan took a deep breath and walked to Miss Bridge's desk.

Luke stood beside it with his hands in his pockets and a smirk on his face. He didn't look worried at all.

"Luke knows he can out-talk Stefan," said Matt.

"And bamboozle Miss Bridges with big fake smiles and big fat lies," said Emily as they headed outside. "I wish we could help Stefan."

"I also wish we had lunch. I'm starving," said Matt. "Come on. Let's check on the sled.

It will help me forget how hungry I am, and I want to report on this place."

Emily and Matt scooted into the shed. As they did, they saw Luke slink out of the classroom and head to the back of the barn.

"Wow! That was fast," said Matt. "I wonder what Miss Bridges said to him and Stefan."

"I hope Stefan is OK," said Emily. "Phew! There's the sled. Just where we left it."

Matt pulled out his recorder. "Ladies and Gentlemen," he began. "Today, Emily and I are students in a one-room prairie school in 1910. We're helping a Ukrainian boy learn English. We're also helping him stand up to a couple of bullies named Luke and Arthur."

"Who said my name?" snarled a voice.

Emily and Matt looked up. Arthur had followed them into the shed. Matt stuffed the recorder into his pocket.

"We were just talking about all the new kids we met at school," said Matt.

"Why did you say 'ladies and gentleman,' as if there were lots of people here?" asked Arthur.

"Oh, Matt always says that. It's a joke," said Emily.

"I don't believe you," said Arthur. "You're up to something."

Just then, Luke ran up behind Arthur.

He walked up so close to Matt that Matt felt Luke's breath on his face. His breath smelled of smoke.

Matt grimaced. "Were you smoking?" he asked.

"Mind your own business," snarled Luke. "You'd better watch out. Arthur and I are going to get both of you. And your dumb friend Stefan, too."

Then he poked Matt in the ribs and took off with Arthur.

9

Hurry!

The bell rang.

Emily and Matt raced toward the school building.

"Luke and Arthur are mean," said Emily as they filed into the classroom.

"We'd better watch them," said Matt. "Who knows what they'll do next?"

"There's Stefan," said Emily. Stefan was sitting at his desk, practicing his printing on his slate board. He looked up when he saw Emily and Matt.

"What happened?" asked Matt.

"Miss Bridges said that since she could not see what happened with Luke's shirt, I should not have to pay for it. She said she would speak to Luke's father. Luke did not like that. He is even angrier with me than before."

"He threatened us at lunch," said Emily. She slipped into her seat as the class marched in. Then she opened her reader.

"Yuck!" she said. A dead black spider was splattered across the page. "I know who did this!"

Emily raced over to Luke's desk. She tapped him on the shoulder.

Luke glanced up. "What do you want?" he snarled.

"I'm not afraid of spiders. And I'm not afraid of you," she said.

Emily turned, but before she reached her

seat, a pebble hit her back. She spun around and stuck her tongue out at Luke.

Then Emily popped back into her seat.

"We have to do something about Luke," she said.

"And we'd better do it soon," said Matt. "He's getting meaner and meaner."

"Class, open your history books and we will take turns reading aloud," announced Miss Bridges.

"Matt, you can share with Stefan again. Luke, begin reading."

Luke cleared his throat. "A long time ago," he began.

"What's that smell?" Stefan whispered to Matt.

"I don't smell anything," said Matt.

"Look!" Stefan pointed out the window. "There's smoke near the barn!"

Stefan leaped out of his seat. "Fire!" he shouted.

The students jumped out of their seats.

"Is it a prairie fire?" cried Melanie. "What if everything

burns!" Melanie sobbed as Stefan raced outside toward the barn.

Emily and Matt ran out after Stefan. They grabbed buckets from the shed, filled them with water from the well, and threw the water at the flames.

"More water! Hurry! Our sled's in the shed beside the barn. We can't let it burn," said Matt.

As Emily and Matt tossed water at the flames, they heard students screaming inside the school. They saw Miss Bridges at the school house door. "Stay calm," she told the students. "Everyone, outside quickly."

The students spilled out of the classroom past Miss Bridges.

"Grab buckets and sacks and help put out the fire," Miss Bridges said. "Quickly!"

Miss Bridges and some of the children filled buckets with water and tossed water on the flames. Others grabbed the burlap sacks piled at the back of the school.

They dipped the sacks in water and slapped them against the flames.

The wind kicked up and blew the flames

higher. Luke's horse neighed from inside the barn.

"Prince is in the barn!" yelled Luke. "We have to save him. We can't let him die. Please. Please help him! I...I didn't mean it. It was an accident!"

10

Faster

Miss Bridges and the children filled bucket after bucket with water from the well as the flames licked the barn walls. They slapped the flames over and over with the burlap bags.

Luke's horse screamed and kicked the walls. The barn shook.

"More water! Faster!" called Miss Bridges, pointing to the barn. "Isaac and Miranda, stand near the firewall around the school with your buckets. We can't let the fire spread!" Miss Bridge's bun came undone as she ran back and forth from the well to the shed and the barn. Her face flushed as she helped the students toss water on the flames.

"My horse is going to die!" wailed Luke. He ran toward the barn door, but the thick smoke forced him back. He fell backward, gagging. He stuck his face in his hands and sobbed. "Please don't let Prince die!"

"I'm going in," said Stefan.

"Don't!" Emily grabbed Stefan's arm to stop him.

But Stefan didn't listen. He shook off Emily's arm, grabbed his handkerchief, and covered his mouth. Then he raced inside the barn.

"Why did Stefan go in?" cried Emily, coughing. The smoke was so thick, she could barely breathe. It was getting hotter and hotter. Sweat was pouring down everyone's face.

Emily mopped her damp forehead with her

hand. She stared at the barn. When was Stefan coming out? It seemed like he'd been in there forever.

Flames leaped out of the small barn window. There was a roar like a gunshot and a piece of the back barn wall crumbled.

"Oh, no!" screamed Emily. "Stefan, come out. Please."

And then, finally, he did. Stefan stumbled out of the barn. His face was covered in black soot. He was leading Luke's terrified horse.

Luke leaped up and ran to his horse. "Oh, Prince," he said. He stroked the horse's soft nose. Then he turned to Stefan. "Thank you," he mumbled.

Stefan nodded. He couldn't speak. He sat on the ground, coughing and trying to catch his breath. His shirt was torn and his shoes were scuffed and grey with ashes.

Emily raced to the well and filled a metal cup with water.

"Here," she said. "Drink this. You were so brave!"

"Stefan, are you all right?" asked Miss Bridges, hurrying over. "You should not have gone into the barn. You could have been burned."

"I am all right," muttered Stefan.

"Look, Miss!" exclaimed Isaac. "The wind has stopped blowing!"

Everyone looked up. They had stopped the fire from spreading, but the barn walls were crumbling. The shed was black with soot, but it was still standing.

Miss Bridges sighed.

"Thank goodness, the fire is out and no one was hurt. I've seen prairie fires spread so fast, there wasn't time to save anything. We owe

Stefan a great thank you for spotting the fire and saving Luke's horse," said Miss Bridges.

"But how did the fire start?" Miss Bridges asked. She walked to the back of what remained of the barn.

"It couldn't be...or could it?" She bent over and picked something up from the charred grass. Then she marched over to Luke and held up the object. It was a burnt pipe.

"Is this yours?" she said.

"I...I didn't th-think anything w-would happen," stammered Luke. "I love Prince. He's the best horse in the world."

"I warned you not to smoke last week," said Miss Bridges. "Your horse almost died. And the school could have burned down." She glared at Luke. His face was wet with tears.

"I'm really sorry, Miss, for...everything," said Luke. "I didn't want anyone to get hurt. Please believe me."

"We will deal with this tomorrow," said Miss Bridges, "It's almost time to go home now. Gather your things, children, and head home. It's been quite a day."

The children walked back toward the school.

"Em, Let's check on the sled," said Matt. "That fire was too close."

Matt and Emily scurried toward the shed.

"Where are you going?" asked Stefan.

"We left something in the shed," said Matt.

Stefan turned toward the schoolhouse.

"Stefan!" called Emily.

Stefan spun around.

"Thank you for everything!"

Stefan smiled and waved. "Thank you," he said. "It's good to have friends."

11

In One Piece

"There it is!" cried Matt. He patted the sled like an old friend.

"It's in one piece, and there are no burn marks anywhere. It's lucky Stefan saw the fire, and the wind died down."

"Come on, Em. Let's get back to the classroom now. I want to ask Miss Bridges if she has an extra sandwich or something. I'm so hungry, I can hear my stomach rumbling like a volcano."

Emily shook her head. "We can't go back to school. Look!"

Shimmery gold words were forming on the front of the sled:

You've helped a friend.
He'll find his way.
But now you must
Fly home today.

"We have to go home," said Emily.

Matt sighed. "I know. But I wish we could say goodbye to Stefan."

"We did just now, sort of, even though we didn't know it was time to go. I'm glad we thanked him. He was—"

"Awesome!" said Matt.

Emily sat down on the sled. "I know he'll be okay now."

Matt nodded. "He sure showed Luke he

wasn't afraid, and he saved Luke's horse."

Matt popped down on the sled. "Ready?"

"Ready!"

Matt rubbed the leaf three times fast.

The sled began to lift up, up over the school-house, over the shed, and over the prairies. Soon they were soaring into the fluffy white cloud.

"Home again!" said Emily as they landed back in the tower room. "You know what I'd like to do?"

"What?" asked Matt, leaping off the sled.

"Learn how to make those pysanky eggs. They're beautiful."

"Stefan said they took hours to make and

they have to use wax and special dyes."

"Well, if they're too hard to make the real way, I could make some paper pysanky and hang them all over my room."

"You know what I'd like to do?" asked Matt.

"What?"

"Eat! I'm so hungry. I'd even eat a spinach salad. And I hate spinach."

"Oh, no!" said Emily. "I think that's all we have in the fridge! I don't think my mom went food shopping yet. She loves spinach."

"Really?" said Matt.

"Yes. She does love spinach...but I was only joking. Mom has more food in the fridge. I think there might be some leftover prairie dog pie."

"Emily!" said Matt. "I'm too hungry for jokes."

Emily laughed.

"Actually," she said, "so am I. Do you want a peanut butter and jelly sandwich?"

And by the grin on Matt's face, Emily knew he did.

MORE ABOUT...

After their adventure, Matt and Emily wanted to know more about the pioneer days, one-room schoolhouses, and pysanky eggs. Turn the page for their favourite facts.

Matt's Top Ten Facts

1. Kids in pioneer days chewed gum made from the sap of spruce trees. Some people said it tasted nasty but they still kept chewing.

Yuck! I bet it was like chewing a tree. -E.

2. Some people on the prairies built sod houses. Sod is thick grass, and it was cut like bricks and piled up.

3. Neighbours often came to help build the sod house and had a "sodding" bee. They sometimes built the whole house in a day. Then they had a party to celebrate.

4. In some places where there were lots of trees, people built log houses. The logs were plastered with mud inside and out. Then they were whitewashed.

5. Lightning started some prairie fires. Dry land burned easily and the wind made the fire spread.

6. Here's what you'd see and hear if there was a prairie fire: flames would shoot up into the sky, and if it was windy, the fire might leap over rivers and move as fast as a racing horse. You'd hear roaring like a hurricane. You'd barely be able to breathe from all the heavy smoke. It would be so scary!

7. Some farmers and schools built fireguards around their property to protect them from fires. They'd plough some land around their property so there was nothing to catch on fire.

8. Many prairie homesteaders complained of terrible mosquitoes in the summer, biting both animals and people.

> The best thing about winter is that there are no mosquitoes. -E.

9. Kids in pioneer days often competed in spelling bees.

10. Pioneer kids played hide and seek, just like they do today.

Emily's Top Ten Facts

1. Ukrainian kids liked Easter for many reasons. They loved the Easter eggs, called pysanky, and they often got new clothes at Easter.

2. Here are some jobs pioneer kids used to do at home: pump the well, carry water, weed the garden, feed the horses, clean the barn, and milk the cow.

3. Some kids began helping when they were as young as three.

4. Some pioneer kids walked miles to get to school. They were lucky if they had a horse to ride all the way there.

5. Some people called outhouses privies.

I call them stink houses.
—M.

6. If you were left-handed in the early 1900s, teachers might force you to use your right hand at school, even if it was really hard.

7. Schools in Canada flew the Union Jack, the British flag. Its three colours were red (for courage), blue (for truth), and white (for purity).

8. Some teachers hit kids with willow switches (a skinny branch from the willow tree) when they misbehaved.

Phew! Miss Bridges didn't have a willow switch. —M.

9. Many country schools shut down from January through March because of bad weather. Kids couldn't get to school or the schools were too cold, even with stoves.

10. One kid said that if you were near the stove in a one-room schoolhouse, you sweated but if you were in the back, you froze.

MORE ABOUT PYSANKY

Ukrainians make beautiful, dyed Easter eggs called pysanky. Archaeologists have discovered ceramic pysanky eggs that go back to 1300 B.C. The word pysanky comes from a Ukrainian word that means to write. Although there's no writing on the eggs, they have patterns and decorations that have special meanings.

Children would often receive pysanky with flower patterns in light colours. Teenagers would get pysanky with lots of white to show that their future was still blank. An older person might get a pysanky decorated with black ladders and gates to remind them that they had a bridge to heaven.

Pysanky used to be made at night by the women in the family while everyone slept. Before she started to make the eggs, a woman was supposed to say only good things about people, be patient, and take special care of her family.

Emily's pysanky

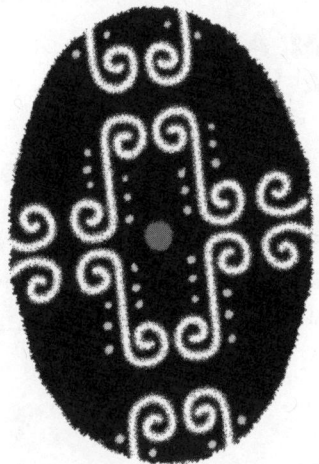

Matt's pysanky

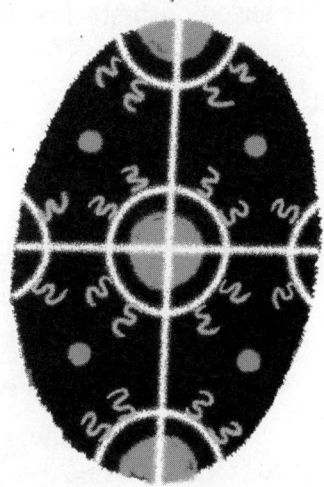

So You Want to Know...

FROM AUTHOR FRIEDA WISHINSKY

When I was writing this book, my friends wanted to know more about pioneer times on the Canadian prairies in the early 1900s. I told them *Pioneer Kids* is based on historical facts but that all the characters are made up. Here are some other questions my friends asked me.

Where is Ukraine?

If you look on a map of Europe you'll see it lying north of the Black Sea between Russia and Poland.

Where did Ukrainians settle in Canada?

Many settled in Western Canada from Southeast Manitoba to Edmonton, Alberta.

Why did people leave Ukraine for Canada?

Poor farmers in Ukraine were looking for a better life and a chance to own land. They heard they could get 160 acres in Canada for ten dollars. It sounded like an amazing deal.

Why did Canada want immigrants?

The Canadian government needed people to farm large areas of land. Many parts of Canada had few people living on it. The government couldn't get enough people from the United Kingdom to immigrate to Canada, so it began advertising in Eastern Europe.

How was the immigrant's trip out west?

Long and hard. It usually started with a long, crowded, and sometimes stormy sea voyage. Then the immigrants had to travel by train across Canada for about a week. The trains were crowded. And they were uncomfortable—people had to sleep on hard benches.

How did the new immigrants find life in Canada?

Tough. The soil was hard to farm, the weather was harsh, and they didn't know the language or the culture. They found the vast, treeless landscape unfamiliar. Many Ukrainians settled near each other, and that helped them feel comfortable. But sometimes they didn't make enough money from farming, and some of the men had to work on the railroad. The women were left behind to run the farm alone.

Why were prairie fires so dangerous?

Prairie fires can spread quickly, especially if there's a wind. Wind makes the fire hard to stop, even with fire-fighting equipment. In Manitoba in the late 1890s, a terrible prairie fire fanned by the wind killed people, animals, and crops. It burned down homes and barns, and destroyed farm tools. If the wind hadn't changed direction, it probably would have caused even greater damage.

How were Ukrainians treated by Canadians when they first arrived?

Some of their new neighbours said they wouldn't fit in because their language and culture was different. The Ukrainians proved them wrong. They worked hard, were excellent farmers, and became good citizens of their new country.

Teacher Resource Guides now available online. Please visit our website at www.owlkidsbooks.com and click on Teacher Guides under Resources/Activities to download tips and ideas for using the series in the classroom.

The *Canadian Flyer Adventures* Series

#1 Beware, Pirates!

#2 Danger, Dinosaurs!

#3 Crazy for Gold

#4 Yikes, Vikings!

#5 Flying High!

#6 Pioneer Kids

#7 Hurry, Freedom

#8 A Whale Tale

#9 All Aboard!

#10 Lost in the Snow

#11 Far from Home

#12 On the Case

#13 Stop that Stagecoach!

#14 SOS! Titanic!

#15 Make It Fair!

#16 Arctic Storm

#17 Halifax Explodes!

More Praise for the Series

"[Emily and Matt] learn more than they ever could have from a history textbook. Every book in this new series promises to shed light on a different chapter of Canadian history."

~ *MONTREAL GAZETTE*

"Readers are in for a great adventure."

~ *EDMONTON'S CHILD*

"This series makes Canadian history fun, exciting and accessible."

~ *CHRONICLE HERALD (HALIFAX)*

About the Author

Frieda Wishinsky, a former teacher, is an award-winning picture- and chapter-book author, who has written many beloved and bestselling books for children. Frieda enjoys using humour and history in her work, while exploring new ways to tell a story. Her books have earned much critical praise, including a nomination for a Governor General's Award in 1999. In addition to the books in the *Canadian Flyer Adventures* series, Frieda has published *What's the Matter with Albert?*, *A Quest in Time*, and *Manya's Dream* with Maple Tree Press. Frieda lives in Toronto.

About the Illustrator

Gordon Dean Griffiths realized his love for drawing very early in life. At the age of 12, halfway through a comic book, Dean decided that he wanted to become a comic book artist and spent every spare minute of the next few years perfecting his art. In 1995 Dean illustrated his first children's book, *The Patchwork House*, written by Sally Fitz-Gibbon. Since then he has happily illustrated over a dozen other books for young people and is currently working on several more, including the *Canadian Flyer Adventures* series. Dean lives in Duncan, B.C.